Who's That Man?

Marny Duncan-Cary & Megan Mansbridge

YOUR NICKEL'S WORTH PUBLISHING

For my late grandparents, who started this story.
For my dad, Gerry. I love you.
For my uncles: Allan, Gord, Jimmy & Roy, who also waited for Grandpa to come home.
For Auntie Judy and Uncle Bill, who arrived after Grandpa's return.

AND

To all the families of the armed services — past and present — who share the same story.

MARNY

To my parents, Christopher and Mary Ellen, for being my first teachers;
my husband, Joël, your love and support provided the space in which these illustrations were created;
my three amazing sons, Zach, Fynn & Theo, for making me a mother;
and to each of you for always giving me the freedom to be myself.
Your contributions are received with love and gratitude.

MEGAN

Foreword

The inspiration for this song came while watching the events of 9-11 on TV. How horrifying it was. I was on the phone with my dad when the second tower came down. We were both in disbelief—was this the news or a movie? I was instantly filled with fear because I knew there would be retaliation, more destruction, more devastation and more war. I was so scared for my children, and I was especially scared for the children and families who would be directly affected.

For me, world war was a thing of the past—nearly forgotten. It was then that my dad reminded me of our family's history with war. My grandpa served in the Canadian Army during the Second World War and was gone from his family for four years. My dad never knew my grandpa until he was five years old. I had known this for a long time but never understood the impact of that separation until 9-11. What happened that day meant that more children and parents would be separated from each other because of war. After several more conversations with my dad about his memories of the day he met his dad, I came up with this song. It's written from a little boy's point of view, and is what I think my dad might have felt on the day his father finally came home.

The song seemed to resonate with audiences and, with the artwork of my beautifully talented friend, Megan, evolved into the book you now hold.

I was playing across the tracks
with my friend, Belle,
catching frogs in the grass,
when I heard my brother yell.

Roaring down the dirt road
like never before, screaming,
"Dad's home! Dad's home!
He's home from the war!"

Who's that man?
Is he my dad?
Does he look like me and
will he love me?

Am I everything he hoped I'd be?
Who's that man?

I ran as fast as I could
in my brown leather shoes.
I'd been waiting my whole life
to finally hear this news.

Out of breath when I got to the back door,
I crept in real slow; excited and scared
and I couldn't wait to know...

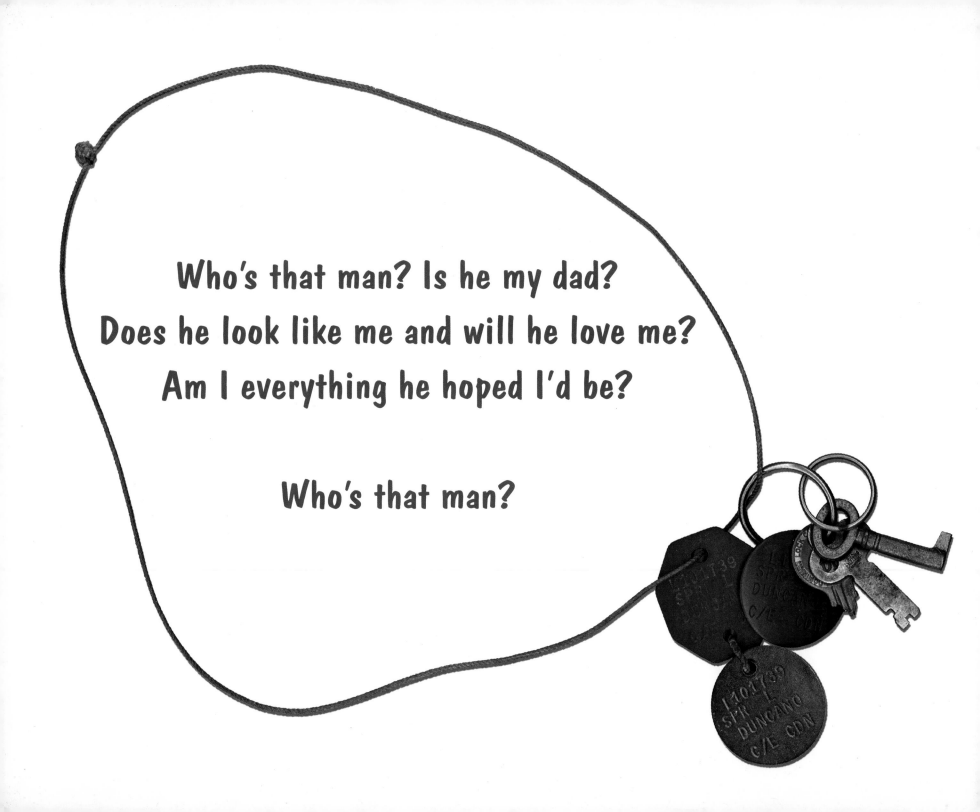

Who's that man? Is he my dad?
Does he look like me and will he love me?
Am I everything he hoped I'd be?

Who's that man?

Leaning on the kitchen counter
in his uniform...

...he'd been called to serve
our country
just before I was born.

He was smiling at me,
but I think I saw a tear.
His voice was faint and broken,
but I heard him say quite clear:

"Who's that boy? Is he my son?
Does he look like me and will he love me?"

"Am I everything he hoped I'd be?
Who's that boy?"

Who's that man? Is he my dad?

Does he look like me
and will he love me?

Am I everything he hoped I'd be?
Who's that man?

Who's That Man?

Words & Music by Marny Duncan-Cary

I was play-ing a-cross the tracks__ with my friend__ Belle,__ catch-ing frogs in the grass__ when I heard my bro-ther__ yell. Roar-ing down the dirt____ road__ like ne-ver__ be-fore,__ scream-ing__ "Dad's home! Dad's____ home!__ He's home from the war!"____ Who's_____ that man? Is he _____ my _____ Dad? Does he look like ____ me____ and will he _____ love ____ me?____

Am I ev' - ry - thing ___ he ___ hoped I'd ___ be? ___ Who's that ___

man? ___ Who's that ___ man? ___

2. I ran as fast as I could in my brown leather shoes—
I'd been waiting my whole life to finally hear this news.
Out of breath when I got to the back door, I crept in real slow;
excited and scared I couldn't wait to know

Who's that man? Is he my dad?
Does he look like me and will he love me?
Am I everything he hoped I'd be?
Who's that man?

3. Leaning on the kitchen counter in his uniform,
he'd been called to serve our country just before I was born.
He was smiling at me, but I think I saw a tear.
His voice was faint and broken but I heard him say quite clear:

"Who's that boy? Is he my son?
Does he look like me and will he love me?
Am I everything he hoped I'd be?
Who's that boy?"

Who's that man? Is he my dad?
Does he look like me and will he love me?
Am I everything he hoped I'd be?
Who's that man?

Author

Marny Duncan-Cary is a singer/songwriter whose music and lyrics convey the heart of her life in southern Saskatchewan. She holds an education degree from the Saskatchewan Indian Federated College at the University of Regina and has since turned her talents to singing and writing songs, releasing her debut album, *Reason For Bein'*, to national critical acclaim and garnering four Saskatchewan Country Music Awards in the process.

Marny lives on an acreage near Lumsden, Saskatchewan with her best friend Trevor, who also happens to be her husband. Together they are enjoying the roller coaster ride that comes with raising bright and beautiful teenaged daughters. *Who's That Man?* is her second book. She can be contacted at www.girlsinger.ca.

Illustrator

Megan Mansbridge was born and raised in rural Saskatchewan. She is a painter, a sculptor and most importantly, a mother, and she combines these gifts to create works that are earthy, honest and that capture all the qualities of a warm home.

Megan graduated from the Alberta College of Art and now lives on the Sunshine Coast of British Columbia with her husband, Joël Fafard, and their three sons: Zach, Fynn and Theo. Megan's creativity is charged by motherhood and the quiet beauty of nature.

Also from Marny Duncan-Cary

Based on the song by Marny Duncan-Cary, *Linger* — a beautifully illustrated book set in the picturesque Qu'Appelle Valley — shares a mother's bittersweet feelings of loss and pride on her child's first day of school.

Available at a bookstore near you or order online at www.girlsinger.ca or www.yournickelsworth.com.

written by Marny Duncan-Cary & illustrated by Megan Mansbridge

"Linger" and "Who's That Man?" can be heard on Marny Duncan-Cary's award-winning CD, *Reason for Bein'*.

Order at your favourite music store or purchase online at www.girlsinger.ca.

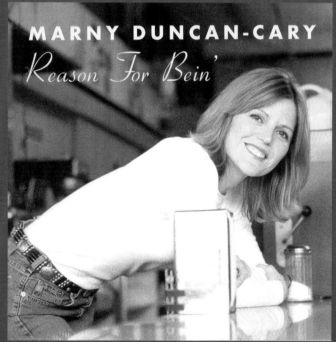

Who's That Man?

Manufactured by Friesens Corporation in Altona, MB, Canada
October 2009
Job #50006

Library and Archives Canada Cataloguing in Publication

Duncan-Cary, Marny, 1967-
    Who's That Man? / Marny Duncan-Cary & Megan Mansbridge.

Based on the song by Marny Duncan-Cary.
ISBN-13: 978-1-894431-38-5

1. World War, 1939-1945—Juvenile fiction.
I. Mansbridge, Megan, 1970-   II. Title.

PS8607.U53W48 2009   jC813'.6   C2009-905905-3

Design: Heather Nickel
DVD production: Jim Nickel
Lead sheet: Craig Salkeld & Dave Chobot
Photos: Duncan family collection

Your Nickel's Worth Publishing
Regina, SK.

www.yournickelsworth.com

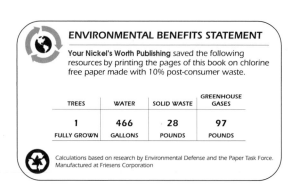

ENVIRONMENTAL BENEFITS STATEMENT

Your Nickel's Worth Publishing saved the following resources by printing the pages of this book on chlorine free paper made with 10% post-consumer waste.

TREES	WATER	SOLID WASTE	GREENHOUSE GASES
1	466	28	97
FULLY GROWN	GALLONS	POUNDS	POUNDS

Calculations based on research by Environmental Defense and the Paper Task Force.
Manufactured at Friesens Corporation

FSC
Mixed Sources
Cert no. SW-COC-001271
© 1996 FSC

A Saskatchewan
Product

Spr L. Duncano served as a military engineer in the Canadian Army from 1942-1946. The medals depicted in this book are his. They are, from top to bottom: the France and Germany Star, the Defense Medal, the Voluntary Services Medal and the War Medal.

Your Nickel's Worth Publishing gratefully acknowledges the contribution of the Saskatchewan Ministry of Tourism, Parks, Culture and Sport through the Creative Economy Entrepreneurial Fund.